THE SONG OF
HIAWATHA

Gilbert

CIP Data is available

Published in the United States in 2003 by Handprint Books

413 Sixth Avenue, Brooklyn, New York 11215

www.handprintbooks.com

First American Edition

Originally published in 2002 in Australia by Five Mile Press

Printed in China

ISBN: 1-59354-002-7

1 3 5 7 9 10 8 6 4 2

THE SONG OF
HIAWATHA

Selections from the poem by Henry Wadsworth Longfellow

Illustrated by Margaret Early

HANDPRINT BOOKS ✋ BROOKLYN, NEW YORK

To the memory of
Michëal Farrell

Publisher's Note

Longfellow's epic poem is far too long to publish in full in a book of
this kind, so excerpts only have been reproduced here (accompanied by
Margaret Early's stunning images). Linking text, which summarizes the
narrative, has been added so children can follow the story, as well as
being exposed to the beauty of Longfellow's classic verse.

Ye who love the haunts of Nature,
Love the sunshine of the meadow,
Love the shadow of the forest,
Love the wind among the branches,
And the rain-shower and the snow-storm,
And the rushing of great rivers
Through their palisades of pine-trees,
And the thunder in the mountains,
Whose innumerable echoes
Flap like eagles in their eyries;—
Listen to these wild traditions,
To this Song of Hiawatha!

The Peace-Pipe

According to American Indian legend, Gitche Manito, the Master of Life,
descended to earth and called together all the warring tribes.

On the Mountains of the Prairie,
On the great Red Pipe-stone Quarry,
Gitche Manito, the mighty,
He the Master of Life, descending,
Stood erect, and called the nations.
"I have given you lands to hunt in,
I have given you streams to fish in,
I have given you bear and bison,
I have given you roe and reindeer,
I have given you brant and beaver,

Filled the marshes full of wild-fowl,
Filled the rivers full of fishes;
Why then are you not contented?
Why then will you hunt each other?
I am weary of your quarrels,
Weary of your wars and bloodshed,
All your strength is in your union,
All your danger is in discord;
Therefore be at peace henceforward,
And as brothers live together."

Gitche Manito said he would send a prophet to live among
them and guide them and teach them.

Wenonah and the West-Wind

Downward through the evening twilight,
In the days that are forgotten,
In the unremembered ages,
From the full moon fell Nokomis,
Fell the beautiful Nokomis,
She a wife, but not a mother.
And Nokomis fell affrighted
Downward through the evening twilight,
On the Muskoday, the meadow,
On the prairie full of blossoms.
"See! A star falls!" said the people;
"From the sky a star is falling!"

There among the ferns and mosses,
There among the prairie lilies,
On the Muskoday, the meadow,
In the moonlight and the starlight,
Fair Nokomis bore a daughter.
And she called her name Wenonah,
As the first-born of her daughters.
And the daughter of Nokomis
Grew up like the prairie lilies,
Grew a tall and slender maiden,
With the beauty of the moonlight,
With the beauty of the starlight.

*Nokomis warned Wenonah not to lie down among the lilies in
case Mudjekeewis, the West-Wind, found her there. But Wenonah did not heed
her mother's warning, and was soon wooed by Mudjekeewis. She later bore him
a son, Hiawatha, but died of grief when the heartless Mudjekeewis deserted her.*

The Infant Hiawatha

By the shores of Gitche Gumee,

By the shining Big-Sea-Water,

Stood the wigwam of Nokomis,

Daughter of the Moon, Nokomis.

Dark behind it rose the forest,

Rose the black and gloomy pine-trees,

Rose the firs with cones upon them;

Bright before it beat the water,

Beat the clear and sunny water,

Beat the shining Big-Sea-Water.

There the wrinkled old Nokomis

Nursed the little Hiawatha.

Old Nokomis used to sing lullabies to her grandson,
Hiawatha, as she rocked him to sleep in his cradle. As he grew older, she
taught him all about the stars and the comets in the sky above, and told him
of the spirits of the warriors.

Hiawatha's Childhood

At the door on summer evenings

Sat the little Hiawatha;

Heard the whispering of the pine-trees,

Heard the lapping of the waters,

Sounds of music, words of wonder;

"Minne-wawa!" said the pine-trees,

"Mudway-aushka!" said the water.

Saw the fire-fly, Wah-wah-taysee,

Flitting through the dusk of evening,

With the twinkle of its candle

Lighting up the brakes and bushes,

And he sang the song of children,

Sang the song Nokomis taught him.

Like all children, Hiawatha was curious about the world
around him. He asked his grandmother about the shadows on the moon, the
colors of the rainbow and the eerie hooting sound in the forest at night.
Old Nokomis taught him all she knew.

Hiawatha's Friends

Then the little Hiawatha
Learned of every bird its language,
Learned their names and all their secrets,
How they built their nests in Summer,
Where they hid themselves in Winter,
Talked with them whene'er he met them,
Called them "Hiawatha's Chickens."
Of all beasts he learned the language,
Learned their names and all their secrets,
How the beavers built their lodges,
Where the squirrels hid their acorns,
How the reindeer ran so swiftly,
Why the rabbit was so timid.

As Hiawatha's days of childhood drew to a close, Iagoo the storyteller
made him a bow and arrow. It was time for Hiawatha to slay his first deer.

Hiawatha the Hunter

Forth into the forest straightway
All alone walked Hiawatha
Proudly, with his bow and arrows;
And the birds sang round him, o'er him,
"Do not shoot us, Hiawatha!"
Up the oak-tree, close beside him,
Sprang the squirrel, Adjidaumo,
In and out among the branches,
Coughed and chattered from the oak-tree,
Laughed, and said between his laughing,
"Do not shoot me, Hiawatha!"
But he heeded not, nor heard them,

For his thoughts were with the red deer;
On their tracks his eyes were fastened,
Leading downward to the river,
To the ford across the river,
And as one in slumber walked he.
Hidden in the alder-bushes,
There he waited till the deer came,
Till he saw two antlers lifted,
Saw two eyes look from the thicket,
Saw two nostrils point to windward,
And a deer came down the pathway,
Flecked with leafy light and shadow.

*Hiawatha swiftly fired his arrow, and then proudly bore the
dead deer home. Old Nokomis made a cloak for Hiawatha from the deer's
hide, and a banquet from its flesh. All the village came to celebrate his feat.*

Hiawatha and Mudjekeewis

*As Hiawatha grew into manhood, he became a skilled
huntsman. He began to ask old Nokomis many questions about his father,
Mudjekeewis. When he learned of his father's falsehood, he decided to travel
to the kingdom of the West-Wind to confront him.*

So he journeyed westward, westward,
Left the fleetest deer behind him,
Left the antelope and bison;
Crossed the rushing Esconaba,
Crossed the mighty Mississippi,
Passed the Mountains of the Prairie,
Passed the land of Crows and Foxes,
Passed the dwellings of the Blackfeet,
Came unto the Rocky Mountains,
To the kingdom of the West-Wind,

Where upon the gusty summits
Sat the ancient Mudjekeewis,
Ruler of the winds of heaven.
Filled with awe was Hiawatha
At the aspect of his father.
On the air about him wildly
Tossed and streamed his cloudy tresses,
Gleamed like drifting snow his tresses,
Glared like Ishkoodah, the comet,
Like the star with fiery tresses.

The Deadly Conflict

For many days Hiawatha listened to his father's boasting
about his past adventures and his courage. At last, Hiawatha's anger rose up
and he accused Mudjekeewis of killing his mother.

And he cried, "O Mudjekeewis,
It was you who killed Wenonah,
Took her young life and her beauty,
Broke the Lily of the Prairie,
Trampled it beneath your footsteps;
You confess it! You confess it!"
And the mighty Mudjekeewis
Tossed upon the wind his tresses,
Bowed his hoary head in anguish,
With a silent nod assented.
Then began the deadly conflict,

Hand to hand among the mountains.
Like a tall tree in the tempest
Bent and lashed the giant bulrush;
And in masses huge and heavy
Crashing fell the fatal Wawbeek;
Till the earth shook with the tumult
And confusion of the battle,
And the air was full of shoutings,
And the thunder of the mountains,
Starting, answered, "Baim-wawa!"

Father and son began to wrestle as the great war-eagle
flapped above them. At last, Mudjekeewis told Hiawatha that he was immortal
and could not be killed. He praised his son's courage and told him to return
to earth and cleanse it of all that harmed it.

The Dark-eyed Minnehaha

Hiawatha set out for home, all his anger gone. He stopped
only once, in the land of the Dacotahs, to buy arrowheads near the falls of Minnehaha.

There the ancient Arrow-maker

Made his arrow-heads of sandstone,

Arrow-heads of chalcedony,

Arrow-heads of flint and jasper,

Smoothed and sharpened at the edges,

Hard and polished, keen and costly.

With him dwelt his dark-eyed daughter,

Wayward as the Minnehaha,

With her moods of shade and sunshine,

Eyes that smiled and frowned alternate,

Feet as rapid as the river,

Tresses flowing like the water,

And as musical a laughter:

And he named her from the river,

From the water-fall he named her,

Minnehaha, Laughing Water.

Warning of Nokomis

When Hiawatha reached the home of Nokomis, he was beset by
many confused feelings. He longed for the lovely Minnehaha.

"Wed a maiden of your people,"
Warning said the old Nokomis;
"Go not eastward, go not westward,
For a stranger, whom we know not!
Like a fire upon the hearth-stone
Is a neighbor's homely daughter,
Like the starlight or the moonlight
Is the handsomest of strangers!"
Thus dissuading spake Nokomis,
And my Hiawatha answered
Only this: "Dear old Nokomis,
Very pleasant is the firelight,
But I like the starlight better,
Better do I like the moonlight!"

Still dissuading said Nokomis:
"Bring not to my lodge a stranger
From the land of the Dacotahs!
Very fierce are the Dacotahs,
Often is there war between us,
There are feuds yet unforgotten,
Wounds that ache and still may open!"
Laughing answered Hiawatha:
"For that reason, if no other,
Would I wed the fair Dacotah,
That our tribes might be united,
That old feuds might be forgotten,
And old wounds be healed forever!"

Hiawatha's Return

Hiawatha returned to the land of the Dacotahs. At the
outskirts of the forest he slew a red deer, flung it across his shoulders,
and sped towards the arrow-maker's wigwam.

At the doorway of his wigwam
Sat the ancient Arrow-maker,
In the land of the Dacotahs,
At his side, in all her beauty,
Sat the lovely Minnehaha,
Sat his daughter, Laughing Water,
Plaiting mats of flags and rushes
Of the past the old man's thoughts were,
And the maiden's of the future.
She was thinking of a hunter,
From another tribe and country,
Young and tall and very handsome,

Who one morning, in the Spring-time,
Came to buy her father's arrows,
Sat and rested in the wigwam,
Lingered long about the doorway,
Looking back as he departed.
Through their thoughts they heard a footstep,
Heard a rustling in the branches,
And with glowing cheek and forehead,
With the deer upon his shoulders,
Suddenly from out the woodlands
Hiawatha stood before them.

The Wooing of Minnehaha

Minnehaha set food and water before the men. She listened
while Hiawatha talked of his home and his childhood. Hiawatha then asked for
Minnehaha's hand in marriage, saying that this would help to bring peace
between his tribe and the Dacotahs.

And the ancient Arrow-maker
Paused a moment ere he answered,
Smoked a little while in silence,
Looked at Hiawatha proudly,
Fondly looked at Laughing Water,
And made answer very gravely:
"Yes, if Minnehaha wishes;
Let your heart speak, Minnehaha!"
And the lovely Laughing Water
Seemed more lovely as she stood there,
Neither willing nor reluctant,
As she went to Hiawatha,
Softly took the seat beside him,
While she said, and blushed to say it,
"I will follow you, my husband!"

And the ancient Arrow-maker
Turned again unto his labor,
Sat down by his sunny doorway,
Murmuring to himself, and saying:
"Thus it is our daughters leave us,
Those we love, and those who love us!
Just when they have learned to help us,
When we are old and lean upon them,
Comes a youth with flaunting feathers,
With his flute of reeds, a stranger
Wanders piping through the village,
Beckons to the fairest maiden,
And she follows where he leads her,
Leaving all things for the stranger!"

Hiawatha's Bride

Pleasant was the journey homeward,
Through interminable forests,
Over meadow, over mountain,
Over river, hill, and hollow.
All the travelling winds went with them,
O'er the meadows, through the forest;
All the stars of night looked at them,
Watched with sleepless eyes their slumber;
Pleasant was the journey homeward!
All the birds sang loud and sweetly
Songs of happiness and heart's-ease;
Sang the bluebird, the Owaissa,
"Happy are you, Hiawatha,
Having such a wife to love you!"
Sang the robin, the Opechee,
"Happy are you, Laughing Water,

Having such a noble husband!"
From the sky the sun benignant
Looked upon them through the branches,
Saying to them, "O my children,
Love is sunshine, hate is shadow,
Life is checkered shade and sunshine,
Rule by love, O Hiawatha!"
Thus it was they journeyed homeward;
Thus it was that Hiawatha
To the lodge of old Nokomis
Brought the moonlight, starlight, firelight,
Brought the sunshine of his people,
Minnehaha, Laughing Water,
Handsomest of all the women
In the land of the Dacotahs,
In the land of handsome women.

Historical Note

"The Song of Hiawatha" was written by the poet **Henry Wadsworth Longfellow** (1807-1882) and published in 1855. I have chosen only a small segment of the poem, hoping it will encourage children to read more of the original. My grandfather read "Hiawatha" to my father in the 1920s, and I in turn read "Hiawatha's Childhood" when I was young. It has been a popular poem for generations in the English-speaking world.

Longfellow found many sources of influence for his poems. The eight-syllable trochaic verse form came from the Finnish national epic "Kalevala". He was also influenced by the tales and legends of the ethnologist Henry R. Schoolcraft (1793-1864), who had married a woman of the Ojibway tribe.

"Hiawatha" is based on the legends about a chief, Manabozho, who is a trickster and fool, as well as a redeemer. Longfellow selected material from Manabozho's adventures but chose to call his hero Hiawatha. Assuming that both names referred to the same person, Longfellow felt that Hiawatha sounded more poetic. However, Manabozho was an Algonquin spirit whereas the man Hiawatha (originally known as Aiontwatha) is part of the Iroquois legend and a tribal god. According to this legend, the Creator sent a Peacemaker named Deganawidah, a numinous figure who traveled amongst the Five Nations (Seneca, Cayuga, Onondaga, Oneida, and Mohawk) in times of war and blood feuds. Together the Peacemaker and Hiawatha persuaded the warring tribes to join a "Great Peace" based on a binding law.

The greatest enemy to peace was Atotarho. His mind was so evil that snakes grew from his hair, and his body was bent in seven places. Because of his magic, no one could approach Atotarho until the Hymn of Peace was composed. He was then hypnotized by the song, allowing Hiawatha to comb the snakes from his hair. (Aiontwatha means "he who combs".) Atotarho's body was then straightened and he became one of the Peace Chiefs. His power was transformed from evil to good and he became the head of the League of Five Nations. Then the fifty chiefs of the Five Nations met on the shore of Lake Onondaga and a white pine was planted as the weapons of war were buried.

—*Margaret Early*